# PLANES

Tony Potter

Illustrated by
## Robin Lawrie

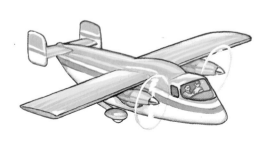

Aladdin Books
Macmillan Publishing Company
New York

# Contents

For Ben and Jamie

First Published in Great Britain 1989
Copyright ©William Collins & Sons Co Ltd 1989

ISBN 0-689-71304-5

Aladdin Books
Macmillan Publishing Company
866 Third Avenue, New York, NY 10022

First Aladdin Books edition 1989

Printed in Singapore

10  9  8  7  6  5  4  3  2  1

CIP data is available

# Inside the plane

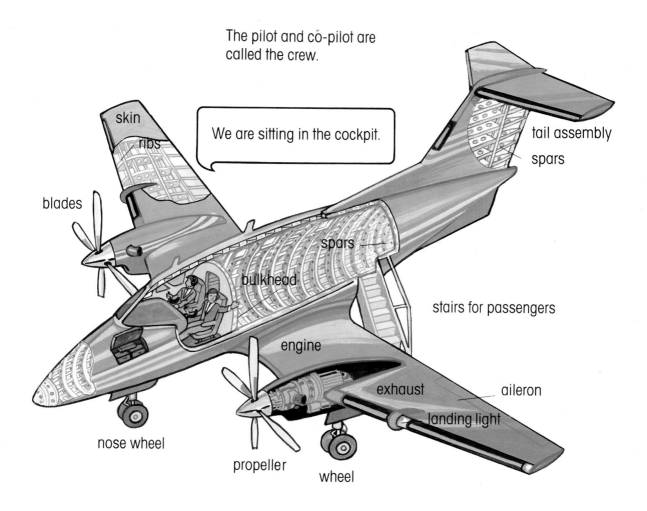

The pilot and co-pilot are called the crew.

We are sitting in the cockpit.

skin

ribs

blades

tail assembly

spars

spars

bulkhead

stairs for passengers

engine

nose wheel

exhaust

aileron

landing light

propeller

wheel

The plane is built around a frame of ribs and spars to make it strong. It has a metal skin.

# Lots of planes

Shorts Skyvan

De Havilland Dash
amphibious plane for land or water

Boeing 737

Concorde

air ambulance

Tristar

turboprop airliner

helicopter

fire-fighting plane

This airport is really busy! Have you ever seen any of these planes?

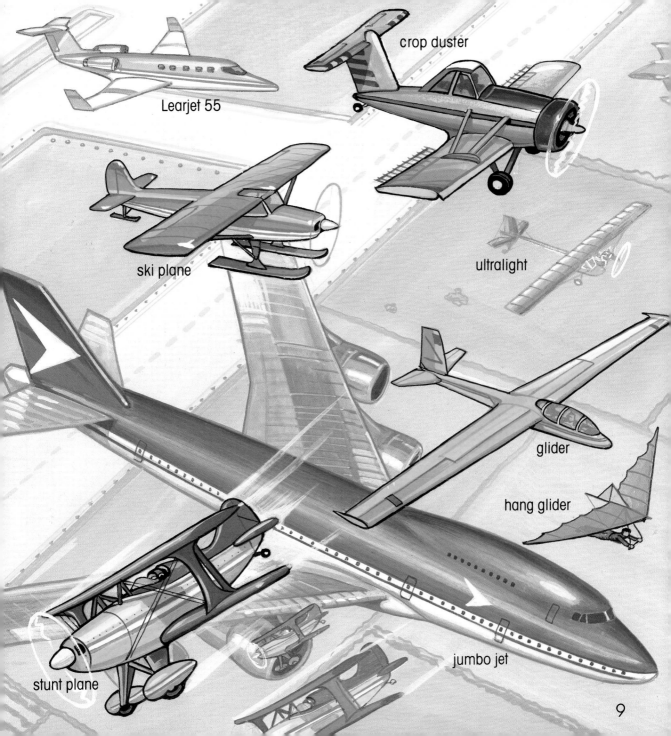

Learjet 55

crop duster

ski plane

ultralight

glider

hang glider

stunt plane

jumbo jet

9

## Kinds of planes

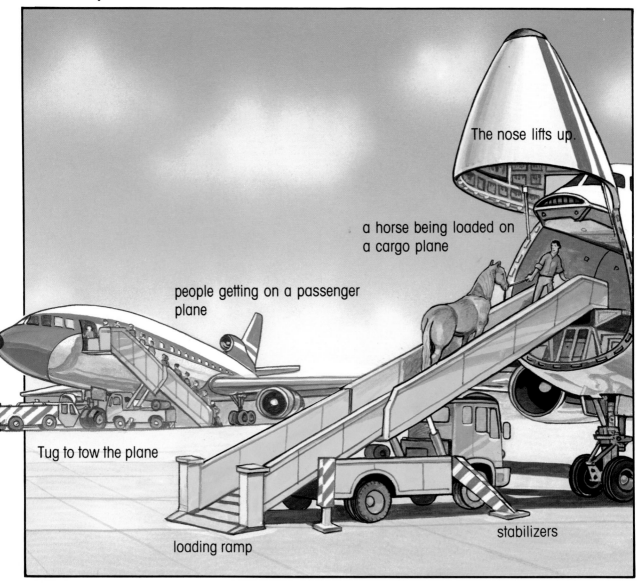

The nose lifts up.

a horse being loaded on a cargo plane

people getting on a passenger plane

Tug to tow the plane

loading ramp

stabilizers

Not all planes are passenger jets. Some are made to transport cargo. Look at the way the nose lifts up on this cargo plane. What are some of the things it might carry?

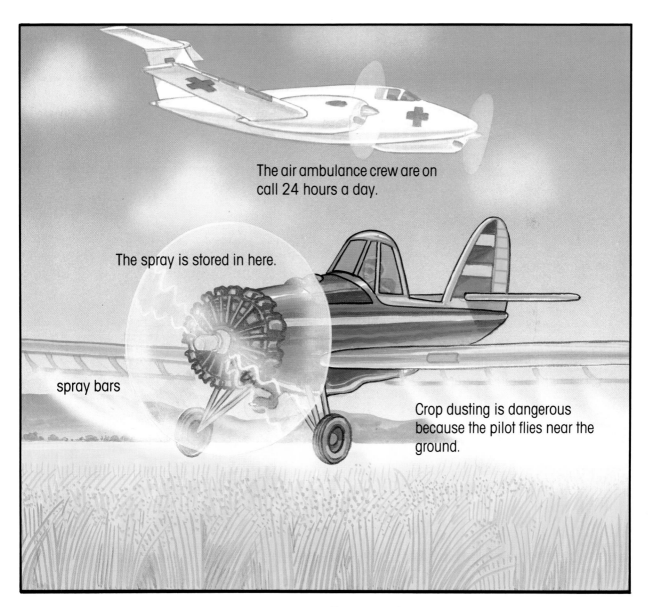

The air ambulance crew are on call 24 hours a day.

The spray is stored in here.

spray bars

Crop dusting is dangerous because the pilot flies near the ground.

There are planes for special jobs, too. Air ambulances take people to the hospital.

Farmers have planes fly over their crops and spray them with weed and pest-killer.

sun visor

captain

weather radar

engine instruments

oxygen mask

Air speed indicator shows the speed.

Artificial horizon shows whether the plane is level.

Altimeter shows how high the plane is flying.

Captain Rogers and his co-pilot are checking their instruments before take-off.

Each pilot has controls to fly the plane. There's also an automatic pilot. It can fly the plane by itself!

12

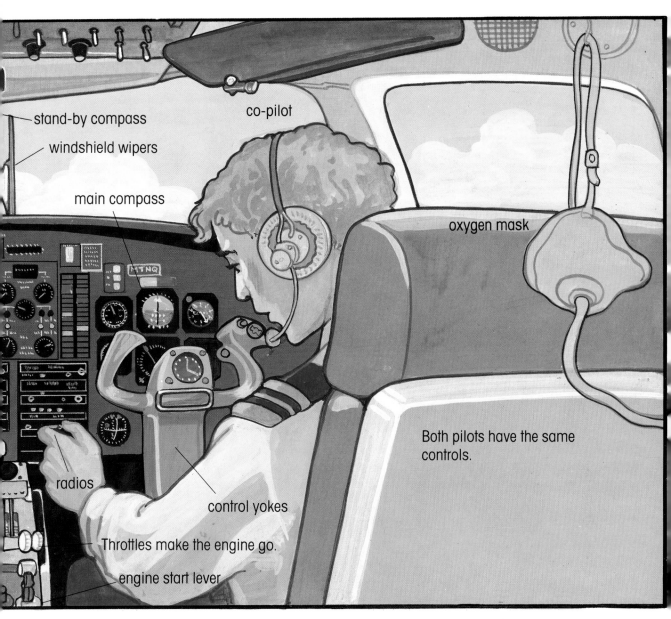

stand-by compass

windshield wipers

co-pilot

main compass

oxygen mask

radios

control yokes

Both pilots have the same controls.

Throttles make the engine go.

engine start lever

The air traffic controller tells the crew when they can start their engines.

He tells them how strong the wind is, and what the weather is like.

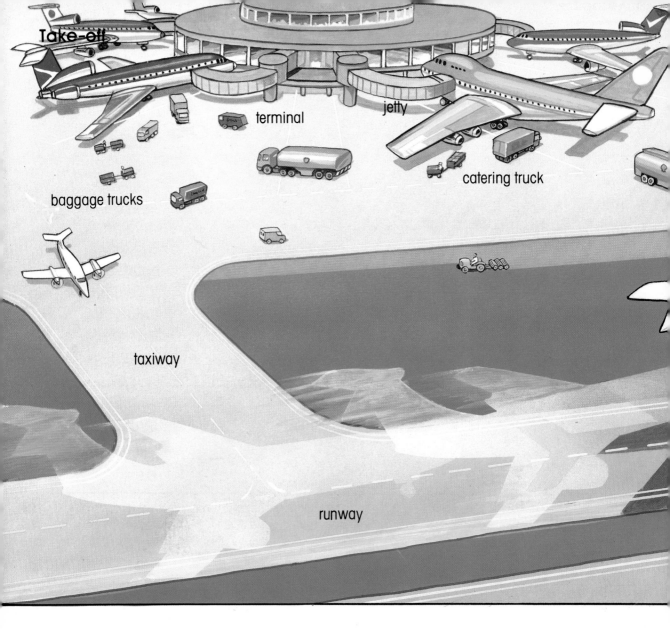

terminal

jetty

catering truck

baggage trucks

taxiway

runway

A passenger jet is taking off down the runway. The pilot has to go at about 160 knots to get off the ground.

This is three times as fast as the speed limit for your car.

14

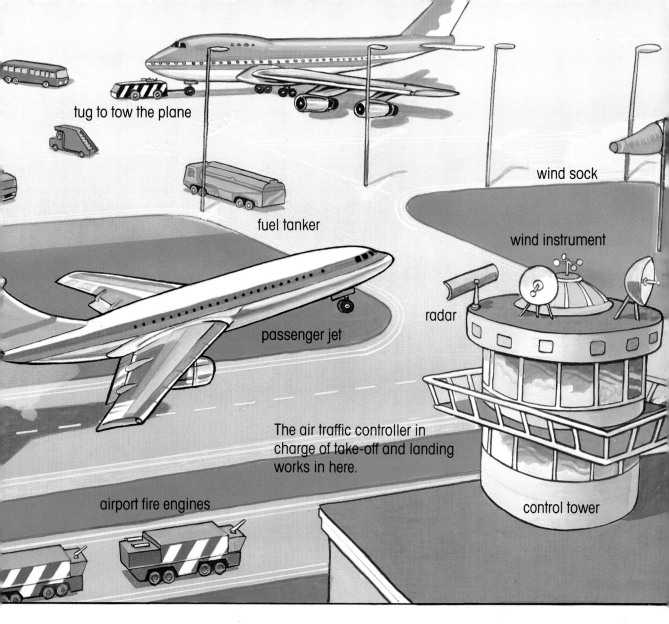

tug to tow the plane

fuel tanker

wind sock

wind instrument

radar

passenger jet

The air traffic controller in charge of take-off and landing works in here.

airport fire engines

control tower

While people wait in the terminal, other planes are being refueled and loaded with baggage.

# Engines

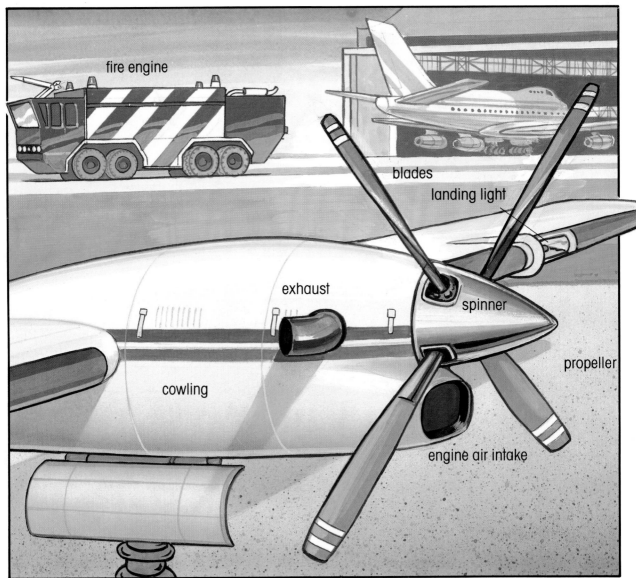

fire engine

blades

landing light

exhaust

spinner

cowling

propeller

engine air intake

Planes have powerful engines to make them go. There are two main kinds: turboprops and jets. Turboprops have propellers to push the air backward and make the plane go forward.

The fuel is stored in the wing.

pylon

fuel tanker

fan

cowl

Technician adjusting the engine

Jet engines use fans to force huge amounts of air through them. Both kinds of engines are powered with fuel mixed with air.

# Flying for fun

wings

This is called a powered hang glider because it has a small engine.

small engine

two-seater

Hang gliders, ultralights and gliders are fun to fly. Lots of people fly them as a hobby.

The pilot controls the hang glider by moving his weight around. Sometimes hang gliders have engines like this one

ultralight

glider

Warm air from power stations
helps gliders to gain height.

Ultralights have an engine and simple
controls.

Gliders are flown like planes, but ride
on warm currents of air without an
engine.

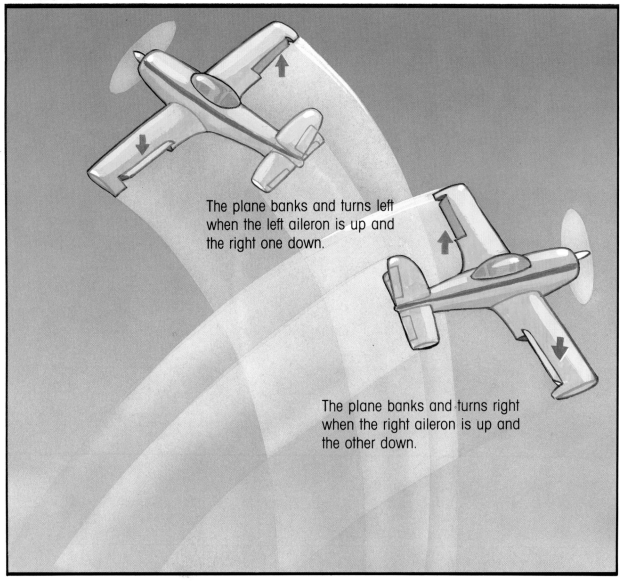

The plane banks and turns left when the left aileron is up and the right one down.

The plane banks and turns right when the right aileron is up and the other down.

Pilots use controls called ailerons to make the plane turn left or right.

The plane tips to one side when it turns. This is called banking.

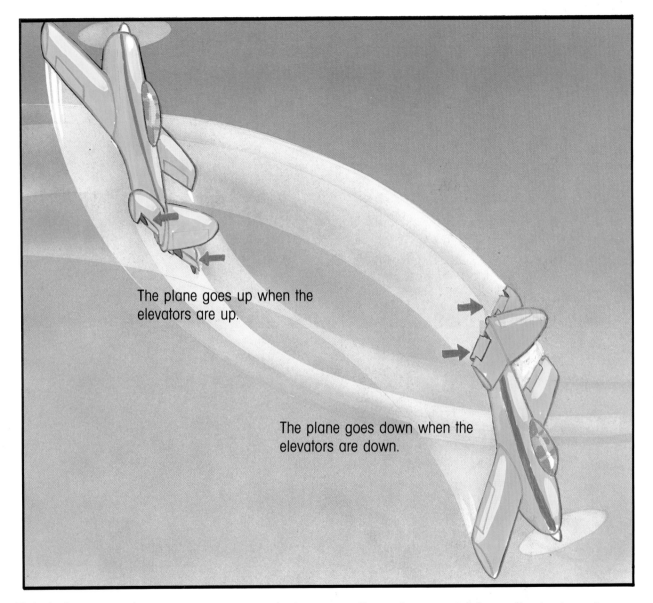

The plane goes up when the elevators are up.

The plane goes down when the elevators are down.

This is how a plane goes up and down. This is called *ascending* and *descending*. The pilot uses controls on the air assembly called elevators to make the plane go up or down.

**aileron:** a flap at the back of each wing to make the plane turn left or right.

**air speed indicator:** an instrument to tell the plane's speed.

**altimeter:** an instrument to tell the plane's height.

**artificial horizon:** an instrument to show the pilot if the plane is flying level.

**cargo plane:** a plane which carries goods instead of passengers.

**crew:** the people who work on a plane.

**elevator:** flaps on the tail assembly that make the plane go up or down.

**fuselage:** the main body of a plane.

**jet:** a kind of engine.

**landing gear:** the wheels and the equipment to raise and lower them.

**passenger plane:** a plane which carries people.

**tail assembly:** the T- or cross-shaped part at the end of the fuselage.

**turbo-prop:** a kind of engine with propellers.

# Index